The Little Chestnut Tree Story

by Lisl Weil

SCHOLASTIC BOOK SERVICES
NEW YORK · TORONTO · LONDON · AUCKLAND · SYDNEY · TOKYO

ISBN: 0-590-04430-3

Copyright © 1973 by Lisl Weil. All rights reserved. Published by Scholastic Book Services, a division of Scholastic Magazines, Inc.

12 11 10 9 8 7 6 5 4

0 1 2 3 4 5/8
07

Printed in the U.S.A.

The Little Chestnut Tree Story

A long time ago, a little sprout of a chestnut tree pushed its way out of the ground.

The sun shone on it.

The rain watered it.

As it grew, it had many friends.

It was a happy tree.

Every year it grew taller and stronger.

In spring, its flowers looked like lovely white candles.

In summer, its leaves made a rich green crown.

In fall, the tree grew nice plump chestnuts.
Everyone had roasted chestnuts to eat
when winter came.

Yes, all year long the chestnut tree had many friends.

In time, people came in horse-drawn carriages to visit the tree.

As more years passed, people built their houses nearby so they could see the beautiful chestnut tree.

Soon there was a whole village around the handsome tree.
People said, "Chestnut Village is really a fine place to live.
And it's only a short ride to the big city."

But the big city got bigger.

It grew closer and closer to the chestnut tree.

In spring, the tree's flowers still looked like white candles.
But they did not stay white for long in the city smoke.

Soon the big, busy city
was all around the
chestnut tree.
And Chestnut Square
became a bottleneck.
"That tree is
bad for our traffic,"
people said.

So the people went to the mayor to complain.
The mayor listened. And he agreed.
The chestnut tree was bad for traffic.

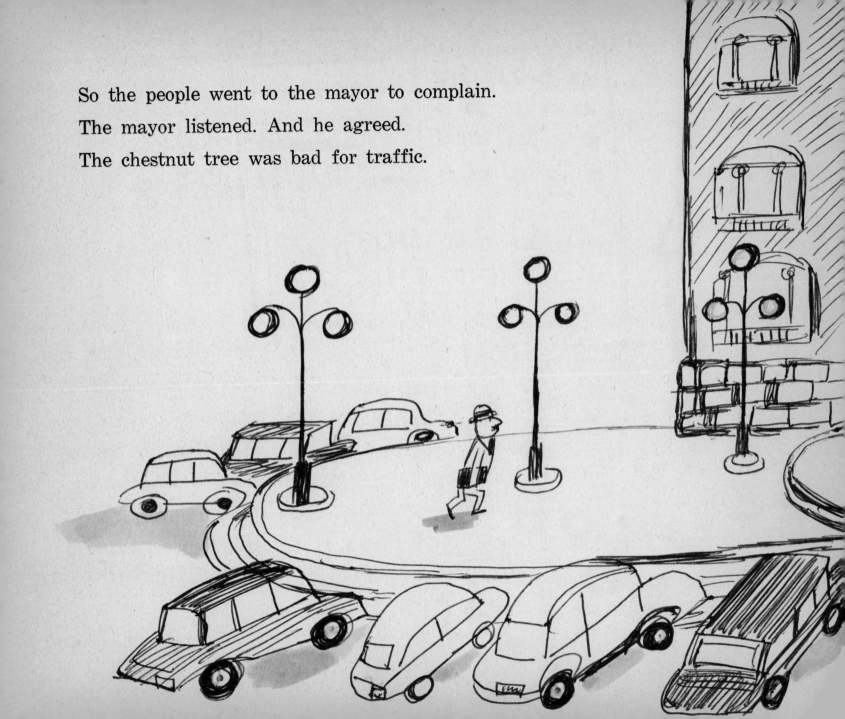

Some weeks later, workmen came with a strong electric saw.
They cut down the beautiful chestnut tree.

But some of its seeds dropped to the ground.
A little bird picked up one seed and . . .

It flew . . .

and flew . . .

until it found a place to plant the seed.

Then a new little sprout of a chestnut tree
pushed its way out of the ground.

And now the story is up to you.